Becoming a Princess

written by Elizabeth Bennett
illustrations by the Disney Storybook Art Team

See the instruction sheet to learn how to use your music player with this book!

White Plains, New York ◆ Montréal, Québec ◆ Bath, United Kingdom

Royal Talent Show

"Gather round!" Miss Flora calls to the kids at Royal Prep.

"We have an important announcement!" adds Miss Merryweather.

"We are going to have a talent show," says Miss Fauna. "And all of you will be in it!"

A talent show! All of the princes and princesses are excited to share their special talents with the school.

3

James will be reciting a poem.
He goes to the library to pick the
perfect poem to read.

Princess Hildegard is thrilled to be playing a piece on the piano.

"I'm so good, I don't really need to practice," she says. But she goes to the music room to rehearse—just in case.

Amber and Khalil are the best dancers in the class. They have decided to perform a dance at the talent show. Off they go to the ballroom to select the right music and dance steps.

Clio is known throughout the land for her baking skills. She decides to bake her special cupcakes to share at the talent show.

Jun knows what she wants to do.
"I just learned a new song on the cello,"
she says. "I will play it for everyone at the
talent show!"

Sofia watches as all of her classmates go off to practice for the talent show. She wishes that she could practice, too, but she doesn't have a special talent. What will she do?

Sofia asks her mom to help.

"I'm sure you will think of something," Miranda tells her. "Think about what you love to do and your talent will shine through."

But planning for the talent show will have to wait. A special guest has come to stay at the castle.

It's Queen Ada and she has brought her pet unicorn, Pearl! Sofia and Amber are so excited!

Sofia and James spend some time getting
to know Pearl. Sofia loves the playful
unicorn. That gives Sofia an idea.

"Maybe I can teach Pearl some tricks
to perform at the talent show!" she says
to James.

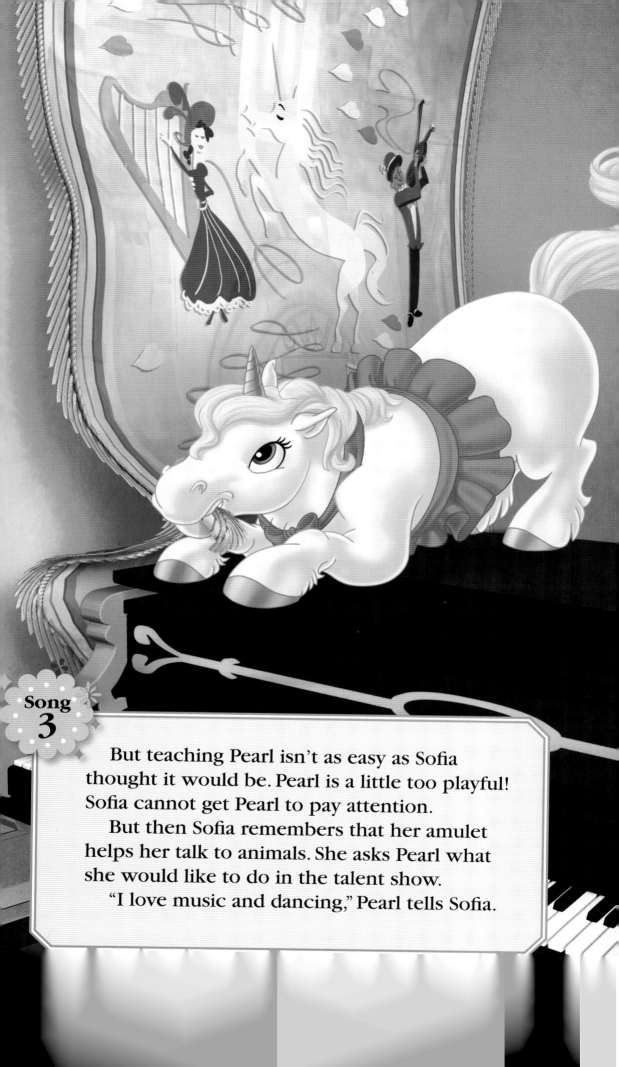

But teaching Pearl isn't as easy as Sofia thought it would be. Pearl is a little too playful! Sofia cannot get Pearl to pay attention.

But then Sofia remembers that her amulet helps her talk to animals. She asks Pearl what she would like to do in the talent show.

"I love music and dancing," Pearl tells Sofia.

Song 4

Now she knows what to do. Sofia teaches
Pearl a dance that they can do together.
She is so proud that she shares it with her
family and their guests. They all agree that
Sofia and Pearl are ready for the talent show!

Song 5

On the day of the talent show, the students perform their special talents for all of their friends and families. Everyone cheers when Pearl and Sofia perform their dance.

Hooray! The Royal Prep Talent Show is a great success!

Sofia and Pearl both know that when you do what you love, your talent shines through!

Song
1

A Proper Princess

Sofia hasn't been a princess for very long and there is so much to learn! Today's lesson is about pouring tea. A proper princess must know how to pour tea correctly.

Sofia tries to pour slowly, but she still makes a mess.

Song 2

"Sometimes I worry that I'll never learn everything about being a proper princess," Sofia says to herself.

Even James knows how to pour tea without spilling! If Sofia is going to be the best princess she can be, she is going to need some help...

"Will you help me?" Sofia asks James.

"Sure!" James tells her. "Come on. I'll show you everything you need to know about tea and table manners. It's easy!" But Sofia isn't so sure.

King Roland knows that there is a lot to learn, but he doesn't want Sofia to worry about learning everything at once.

"Just do your best," he reminds her.

That makes Sofia feel better, but now that she is a princess, she wants to behave like a proper princess.

Except when she is with her
animal friends—then she can
truly be herself and just have fun!

Now I Can Dance

Sofia's first royal ball is just a week away. She is very excited, but she is also worried. She doesn't know how to dance.

"There's nothing to worry about," James tells her. "I can teach you."

James and Sofia don't realize that Amber has been watching them.

Amber has always been the best dancer in the castle and she wants to keep it that way! She decides to play a trick on Sofia.

"Oh, Sofia," Amber calls to her new sister. "I thought you might like to borrow my special dancing slippers for the ball."

"Thank you, Amber!" Sofia says.

Sofia is happy that her brother and sister want to help her get ready for the ball. She continues to practice for her first dance.

But Sofia doesn't know that the dancing slippers have a spell on them. Instead of making her a better dancer, they make her trip and fall! Now Amber is sure that she will be the best dancer at the ball.

When Sofia and Amber get ready for the ball, Amber accidentally rips her gown. "Oh, no!" Amber cries when she sees the rip.

"Just give me a minute and I'll sew it for you," Sofia tells her sister.

In no time at all, Amber's dress looks as good as new.

Song
4

Sofia's kindness makes Amber feel bad about the trick she has played on Sofia. She realizes that she and Sofia can both be the best dancers at the ball.

"Wait, let's practice a little more together," Amber says to Sofia.

With Amber's help, Sofia glides across the floor.

And when the ball begins, Sofia takes her place on the dance floor with King Roland. Together they dance around the room. Everyone has a wonderful time at the ball—even Amber, who is very proud of her sister Sofia.